All They Want for Christmas

All They Want for Christmas

A Novella

Book 1 in The Magnolia Hills Garden Club Series

By
Christa Allan

Cover Design: Melissa Ringette
For information contact:
christa@christaallan.com

Follow Christa on Facebook:
www.facebook.com/ChristaAllan.Author

Follow Christa on Twitter:
http://twitter.com/ChristaAllan

Sign up for Christa's Newsletters:
http://www.christaallan.com

To my daughter, Erin Simonson, for her persistence, honesty, and generous heart. She totally underestimates her talent as a writer. And, thank you to Andrae, her husband, for being on the other end of the time and trouble invested in making this a reality. Jenny Jones, my ever-faithful writer BFF, who answers her phone even when she knows it's me.

Kristen Billerbeck and Sibella Giorello my cyberspace voices of wit, wisdom and "WTH?"

My constant cheerleaders and ever-patient children Michael, Shannon, Sarah and John. My husband, Ken, for, well, everything.

Chapter One

I T TOOK BEULAH GRACE SCHWARTZ three tries, but she finally killed my mother.

The first time was in June when she accused my mother Nancy Jane Pressfield, of diverting $29.54 from the Magnolia Hills Garden Club into her personal account. For fertilizer. Momma told her she was the one full of crap because that money was approved for reimbursement by the treasurer herself, Claretta Morgan, also the CPA for half the town.

Beulah Grace's second attempt was in September when she told her every other Tuesday afternoon bridge group my mother tried to seduce her husband, Ronald Reagan Schwartz. This based on Ronald telling her Nancy Jane brought a Brownie Batter Chocolate Chip Cheesecake to his hardware store to thank him for rekeying all her locks. After momma heard the story from her friends at the Ladies Church Auxiliary, she informed Beulah Grace that if she wanted to look at something old, small and wrinkled, she'd stand buck naked in front of her full length mirror.

Finally, Beulah Grace did her in for good. She denied it, of course. But everyone knew she wasn't only capable of such a murderous act, she'd know exactly how to carry it out.

That morning the sickening alarm of our cat Job, who was screeching like two hells, bolted me out of bed. I closed my eyes for a quick prayer. "Oh, dear God, did she hit him with the riding mower again?" I opened my eyes to peek through the wooden mini blind in my bathroom. But I didn't see or hear the engine racing in the back yard, so it couldn't be another mower mishap. Job lost a smidge of his tail in that one. I grabbed my cell phone off my dresser and started toward the kitchen when an alien noise shattered through Job's cries. It had to be coming from the front yard.

I threw on my coat, even though it was December in south Louisiana, which didn't bite. It mostly just showed its teeth. Besides, no one in Magnolia Hills in their right mind (which excluded half the population) went in their front yard wearing flannel pjs.

Before I opened the front door, I had my

thumb ready to hit 911 on my phone because even in our small town we could never be too careful. If it wasn't Bob Jefferson's cows meandering down the sidewalk because his kids left the cattle gate open, it was 89-year-old Mrs. Casnave next door climbing her ladder to pick kumquats and missing a rung on the way down.

Kneeling on the cold ground, her hair still in spongy curlers and wearing her faded chenille robe, was Momma. Her arms wrapped around her prized Yuletide Camellia plant. What leaves remained on the plant, trembled along with Momma's sobs.

"She's dead. She's gone. Gone."

Her voice sounded like it was being dragged over gravel. Sitting on the pavestone walkway snaked around the cluster of camellia bushes, Job swiveled his head in my direction, then padded off as if to say, "Good luck. She's yours now."

Momma looked at me, her eyes steaming, her cheeks damp from her tears. "She killed her. I know she did. That damn Beulah Grace Schwartz. She poisoned her. I just know it."

She moaned and shook her fist at the heavens.

God had been officially put on notice.

Poor God.

Poor me.

This battle between my mother and her Magnolia Hills Garden Club nemesis Beulah Grace was made all the more complicated by the recent ending of the upcoming nuptials—mine, specifically—to one Jeremiah Levi, the sole surviving son of Beulah Grace and Ronald Reagan Schwartz.

Six months earlier, I'd just signed the loan agreement to open the Mad Batter Bakery along with my partner Preston Atticus Monroe, my best friend since our sandbox days at Miss Lucy's KinderCare. Then, one month later, Youngblood Engineering offered Jeremiah—or Levi as I called him, ignoring his mother's sour expression when I ignored his first name—a new position with a higher salary to help open their new Houston office.

If Preston and I hadn't already signed a two-year-lease on the only available property fronting Main Street, a newly restored Victorian with a porch wide enough to accommodate tables and chairs, and a spacious kitchen for our equipment, I might have been a tad less bitchy about the whole idea of a transfer. Maybe I would have said, "Can we talk about this later?" when he broke the news while I was painting the front room alternating wide strips of butter yellow and frosted mint. Instead, according to Preston who had been rearranging the display cases channeling his inner Nate Berkus, Oprah's home designer guru, my head had swiveled exorcist-like on my neck right before I spewed, "Levi, if brains were leather, you wouldn't have enough to saddle a June bug. Are you kidding me? Move to Houston? Can you see what I'm doing here?"

"What I see, Holly," Levi had said, yanking the knot out of his tie and undoing his collar button, "is me walking out of here, going home to watch tonight's football game, drink beer, and probably fall asleep before halftime ends because I'm so damn tired. I don't even have the energy to fight with you right now."

Preston had walked over and shook Levi's hand. "Well, then, let me be the first to congratulate you," he said, stabbing me with a quick cut of his eyes.

"Thanks, Pres," Levi said, a tired smile appearing. "You're welcome to join me."

Preston grinned. "You know I'd only be sitting there to watch the tight ends' tight ends and relieve you of a few beers." He sighed. "I have to admit, though, the announcers can be so much fun. Talking about penetration and loose balls and going deep," he said. "But I appreciate the invitation. I'll take over for Michelangelo's sister here, so she can go home and have a"—he paused and looked at me—"civilized conversation with you."

That conversation was as wild as my hair on a high humidity day. While I was proud of Levi, I was also frustrated. He could be an engineer anywhere. Opening the Mad Batter Bakery in such a prime location could not. Levi, who needed to relocate in six weeks, which meant about four months before our eve of Christmas Eve wedding, said I didn't have to move there until after we were married. He generously offered to "let" me work at the bakery during the week and travel home on weekends "for a while."

"Seriously? We're going to start our marriage seeing each other on weekends?" I ranted on about my opinion not mattering to him now, so it would be unlikely to ever matter to him. I'd fallen in love with Levi in fourth grade when he told his friends I could shoot a basketball better than he could, and if I wasn't on their team, I'd beat them on the other team. It wasn't until after we both returned to Magnolia Hills after college that our lifetime of friendship made being a couple as easy as breathing.

The rest of the night and for a week after that, we threw words at one another like flaming arrows. Levi and I made love and fought with equal passion. In less time than it took to decide on paint colors for the bakery, we were un-engaged. We accused one another of the same relationship crimes. Selfishness, stubbornness and senselessness.

Two weeks later, I moved out of his house, the one that was supposed to become our house, and he moved to Houston two weeks earlier than he needed to be there. Our mothers, who lived across the street from one another, moved to the land of denial. Convinced we were going through the pre-wedding jitters, they refused to cancel the church, the caterer, the cackling among themselves. When Levi and I still hadn't re-engaged ourselves by September, they relented. Since then, the Magnolia Hills Garden Club threatened to excommunicate them both if they didn't stop enlisting members for Team Levi or Team Holly.

So, less than four weeks before what would have been my wedding day, I'm tugging my mother into the house with one hand and, with the other, speed dialing my father who was still inside, probably only pretending to be asleep, to help me before she broke loose and tore across the street to Beulah Grace's.

I didn't tell my mother I spotted Levi's mother standing behind her screened door, arms folded, wearing a toothy smile and a Santa hat.

Christmas must have come early for Beulah Grace.

Chapter Two

ᐯᑏᐯ

THE LAST TIME I WITNESSED this degree of self-pity in Momma was when my younger sister Lily, born on Easter, came home from LSU with a baby bump instead of a college degree. After the bump was born, Lily and John Jay Winston married in our back yard and moved with triple J (John Jay, Jr.) back to Baton Rouge. John's mom took care of her new grandson so Lily and her husband could finish school. They graduated last year, and with his father's blessing and backing, John opened a restaurant near the college campus that's doing so well, Lily is now home with triple J. Momma, of course, now acts as if she orchestrated the entire series of events that led to the happy ending.

My father reminded her of that in the middle of her mourning over the camellia. "For Gawd's sake Nancy, remember you got triple J out of what you thought was the end of the world. And Lily still got that college degree we sent her there to get. That camellia bush won't make the difference between your winning the Christmas Garden of the Month or not. You got about two dozen other ones scattered all over the damn place."

"That's just not the point, Hamilton." Momma cracked an egg against the stainless steel bowl, flicked her wrist and grabbed another. "Winning this month means I could get picked to attend the Deep South Annual Garden Club Convention in Birmingham next year."

"You're getting mighty worked up about a trip to Alabama." He refilled his coffee mug, winked at me, then said, "Tell you what . . . save all the money you'd spend winning this damn contest, and I'll take you there myself."

"And that's not the point, either." She checked the bacon in the microwave, and set the timer for two more minutes. She swatted him with her dish towel. "I swear, you could give aspirin a headache. Go make yourself useful."

"I'm trying, honey, but I can't get you to leave the kitchen." He sipped his coffee, but his eyes were laughing for him.

Momma swatted him again, a bit harder this time, and reached for yet another egg.

"Um, who's coming over for breakfast? That's

the tenth egg you've used." I said, then scooted out of her way in case the eleventh one landed on my head.

"Never you mind. If you hadn't chased away that fiancé of yours, you wouldn't be here asking that question. And I wouldn't be dealing with his spiteful mother." She grabbed the whisker and violently beat the eggs, her sponge curlers rocking on her head.

"Oh, so we're going to make your dead flowers my fault?" I whopped the can of biscuits in my hand against the kitchen counter, giving Job yet another reason to yowl. "And, no, I'm not making biscuits from scratch this morning." I plopped them on the baking sheet one by one. "You're telling me all Beulah needs to win is for you to lose one camellia bush? Seems to me you're handing over a whole lot of power to that woman."

The egg whisking stopped. "Hamilton, talk to your daughter."

I laughed. "I'm thirty-three, not three," I said as I slipped the biscuits into the oven. "If you don't think you can win, just drop out of the contest."

"You're almost thirty-three. Don't age me before my time." My dad kissed me on my forehead. "You were the best Christmas present ever. Shopped for you nine months earlier, and I didn't even have to wrap you." My father picked up Job. "And now, the men folk are going to the family room. We're not participating in this."

Against the backdrop of the eggs sizzling as they covered the frying pan, Momma said, "Not all of us quit just because things aren't going the way we want."

"GIRLS' NIGHT OUT couldn't have happened at a better time," I told the three women at the table as we popped open our second bottle of Smith & Hook at The Whine Bar.

"You said the same thing when we met the night after Levi moved to Houston." Allee poured a glass and handed it to me. "And the week after you moved back to your parents' house. And after Levi's mother accused you of ruining her son's life . . ."

"Oh, now look what you've gone and done. Made the poor girl laugh," said LamarAnn, her twin, whose sense of humor distinguished her from her look-alike, radically serious sister. That and the fact that one of them parted her mostly-blonde hair on the left and the other on the right.

"I'm a walking 'if I don't laugh, I'll cry' cliché," I said watching the wine slosh against the edge of the glass as I twisted the stem between my thumb and forefinger. "My mother is convinced

Beulah Grace is undermining her, the bakery's supposed to open the week before Christmas, and we're still waiting on inventory that's delayed because it's coming from snow-covered places."

And almost daily I couldn't overcome the compulsion to stare at my wedding dress. I searched for months before Levi had even officially proposed and, when I found it, fell—no, plummeted—into love. The gown was made of champagne tulle with lace appliqués beaded with Swarovski crystals, a pattern repeated on the long lace sleeves. The neckline was wide at the front with a plunging scalloped back. The eight-foot tulle veil was trimmed with lace, then bloomed into a cascade of lace flowers on the lower half. I'd envisioned my mother zipping me into it and Levi zipping me out, the dress collapsing into a puddle of glittering soft spun sugar at my feet.

Mia, my was-to-be matron of honor, snapped her fingers and waved her hand in front of my face. "Hey, are you with us? I asked you where Preston was, and if we should wait on him before we order."

"Sorry," I said and blinked away my walk down the aisle. "He's going to be running late. He's at the bakery waiting on a piece of equipment to be delivered."

"Is that some quirky way of telling us he has a

date?"

"Allee, don't try to be amusing, honey. It doesn't wear well on you," said LamarAnn. "Leave the funny to me." She sipped her wine, and nodded toward her sister. "So, what she said. Is it?"

"The last place Preston would try to hook up with someone would be in the middle of town," said Mia. "Just because the man may be drop-dead gorgeous, built like a linebacker and have skin the color of melted caramel, doesn't mean he's foolish."

"You do know that being hot for Preston is absolutely pointless, plus you're married," Allee said, uncorking a new bottle.

"Which is exactly why I can appreciate his amazing body," said Mia.

We'd adopted Preston into our Girls' Night Out years ago. That he looked as if he could be our bodyguard was sufficient to keep most of the town's hens from clucking. Preston joked no man in the Deep South was "fully" gay, especially a black man. "We just walk lightly or take after our mama's side of the family or become interior decorators. Or hair stylists," he told us one of the night. "Of course, I can't believe these women around here don't have a clue. After all, who did they call to host the 'Swags and Wreath Work-shop' when the guest presenter from New Orleans had the shingles? *Moi.* And, poor Mrs. Neidermeyer, having a hissy fit because she didn't understand why 'that lovely lady cancelled on us to get roofing materials.' "

Allee tapped LamarAnn's hand, and they looked over my shoulder, their eyes like camera lenses zooming in on a target.

"What's going—" I tried to turn in my chair, but Mia put her arm around my shoulder.

"Don't turn around. Preston just walked in with his 'equipment,'" she whispered.

But too late.

Following Preston into the Whine Bar was a tall, well-built man, his black hair, once unruly was now tamed into a short side-part. A man whose beard scruff Holly distinctly remembered brushing against her body.

Jeremiah Levi Schwartz.

Chapter Three

IF MY MEMORY HAD BEEN wiped clean, and Levi was a stranger, I would have fallen in love with him still. Initially, maybe just tripped into lust watching him move across the room, a man comfortable in his own skin. A man whose skin I had grown comfortable being next to, or under, or over at night. The skin my hands memorized. Like the raised scar at the base of his spine where he'd had surgery in college. The mole on the left side of his body, directly above his hip bone.

I hadn't seen or talked to him in over three months. Not counting the night I drunk dialed him after the first month we'd been apart. Preston had dropped me off at home around midnight after we'd had a long, late, mostly liquid dinner. I slipped into bed, fully clothed, wiggled my cell phone out of my jeans' pocket and hit JLS. He wisely didn't answer, but that didn't deter me from leaving a rambling, sloshy monologue that ended with me asking him if ex-engaged couples could have phone sex.

He didn't respond. A choice much wiser than the one I'd made the night before.

When Preston and Levi stopped to talk to the bartender, I looked at my friends at the table. "Raise your hand if you're an accomplice."

The three of them stared at me as if I'd just thrown my wine in their faces.

"We're the ones who asked you about Preston," said Mia. "And you know, I'm a terrible liar, so no way could I have pulled off that question without making you suspicious."

The twins nodded. "Mia's right. She ruined every surprise party we've ever tried to throw," said LamarAnn.

"The only way to pull one off is to make it a surprise for her too." Allee refilled her wine glass. "Look, if Preston had told us he planned this, we would have gone somewhere else."

"After telling him what a crappy idea we thought it was," added LamarAnn. "Where do you think you're going?"

I'd stood up, drained my wine, grabbed my purse and prepared to jet before Preston and Levi wandered over to us. "Home. I'm going home." My trembling voice betrayed the stoic posture I attempted. My brain was engaged in a tug-of-war with my heart, but I wasn't sure they wouldn't conspire against me. Throwing the rope around Levi and pulling him toward me.

"Hmmm. I don't think so, sister," said Allee.

I slung my purse over my shoulder. "Don't be ridiculous. Whether I stay or go is my decision—"

"Well, no, it isn't really." Allee held up a set of keys. "We picked you up."

"Damn." I pressed my fingertips to my lips. "Let me take your car, and you . . ." Three pairs of eyes shifted away from me to over my shoulders. "They're walking this way, aren't they?" No "butterflies in my stomach" cliché for me. Bees, angry swarming bees that stung.

"This is awkward," Mia mumbled. "Kill me now for making fun of Harry Potter and that cloak of invisibility."

I closed my eyes and willed myself to peace, serenity and all that other crap that was supposed to be honey to those damn bees in my gut.

"Hey, betches. So sorry for being late to the party. I waited longer for that oven than Kim Kardashian's marriage lasted to that basketball player." I recognized Preston's "nice-nice" voice. The sing-song one he used to diffuse uncomfortable situations. Like this one. I still hadn't turned around to face him or Levi. Preston tugged at my purse straps. "You on your way in or out?" He bent down and hugged me, tighter than usual, and whispered, "Didn't plan this."

Did I dare admit I didn't know if I was coming or going? Give Levi more evidence of my acting like a human boomerang at times? Concentration was an ocean in my mind. It ebbed and flowed.

"Both," I answered and slid into the chair where I'd been sitting, making eye contact with Levi impossible unless he walked around the table. Which, because I must have ticked off Lady Luck at some point in my life, was the only space with two empty chairs.

"And look who stopped by to see us at the bakery," said Preston, still on the verge of singing, until he said "us" then stared at me. "I told him I was on my way to Girls' Night Out, but he practically insisted he wanted to tell all you fine women 'hello.' "

Levi sat right next to him, so Preston must have counted on his not detecting the raised eyebrows and slight head tilt that conveyed enough information that he could enter a plea of "not guilty."

The waitress appeared, an early Christmas miracle angel, to save us from ourselves. The girls and I greeted her with such relief disguised as enthusiasm, she must have wanted to reconsider offering us more wine. "Another bottle and two more glasses?" She smiled at Preston and Levi as she set napkins in front of them.

"Nothing for me, thanks," said Levi. "I won't be staying long."

I couldn't not look at him. Especially when, before I saw him scan my face, I felt his eyes on me. I lifted my head and looked into the face of the man who let me buy Park Place knowing I'd win, the man who brought me coffee, the newspaper, and three strips of bacon—one shorter where he'd taken a bite—in bed on any given weekend morning. The man who undressed me with his eyes as he unbuttoned my silk blouse, leaving a trail of kisses that started in the hollow of my neck.

"Holly." He nodded.

I nodded. "Levi."

It was a start.

Chapter Four

⁓

LAMARANN LOOKED AROUND THE TABLE as we each silently conceded to her being the one to crack the silence. She tilted her head toward Levi. "Sooooooo, how's Houston?"

"Busy," he replied, his eyes locked on my face.

"Uh huh. Well. . ." LamarAnn elbowed her sister, who elbowed her back and stayed mute.

My brain tightened its reins. "No. No. NO. DO NOT SPEAK." My heart bellowed, "Go for it! Go for it! NOW!" I wanted both to shut up. I bit my lower lip and under the table started picking my fingernails.

"My cousin lives in the Heights—" Mia said.

"Stop. No more BS. We all know why I'm here." Levi stood and slipped his hands into the front pockets of his jeans.

I pretended to study the graffiti carvings on the table. "Lizzie hearts herself" and proclamations of love lost and found.

"Holly?"

A thought shot through my mind that nailed my brain and heart to the wall. *What if he met someone else? Impossible, right? But alone in a new city for three months is a long time.* I shivered. *Maybe he's not here for me. He's here for her.*

"Holly?" A bit louder this time. "Can you please look at me?"

Mia pinched my arm. And not in a figurative sense. I expected a bruise later. "Hey, pay attention here," she said.

I wanted to tell her his voice saying my name was like an unexpected gift. That what I wanted was for the last four months to be a crease in the fabric of time, so December could follow July, and we could make big deals out of little deals like where we were going for dinner that night. And we'd be Levi and Holly planning our lives together.

"Yes," I said, breathing the word out. I looked up into eyes the shade of pecan shells with specks of black. Eyes that, at that moment, swallowed me whole.

He leaned toward me, his hands on the table. "I want to talk to you. Can we go somewhere and make that happen?"

"Now?"

Mia kicked me under the table.

He stared at the table and looked back at me in mild amusement. "I drove here in less than five hours, risked speeding tickets, negotiated Baton Rouge on the night of a football game . . . so, yes, now."

LEVI WALKED AHEAD of me as we left, threading us through the maze of table and the human forest around the long copper-covered bar. He glanced back at me a few times, I guessed to assure himself I hadn't bolted in the opposite direction.

He stopped when we were outside. "I forgot to ask. Is your car here?"

"No, the twins picked me up from the bakery."

"Do you want to get it now or later?"

"That depends," I said, moving away from the door swinging open as people I hoped didn't recognize either one of us left and entered the bar. Magnolia Hills hotline disseminated information faster than Miley Cyrus twerked. And usually with the same range of responses from agony to ecstasy. By tomorrow, the two of us simply standing together outside The Whine Bar could be a tale of a hidden marriage or two and/or a baby.

"We're blocking the doors, and the wind's picking up," he said. "Let's walk to my car, and then you can tell me your conditions."

I followed him in the parking lot, and when he stopped at a car I didn't recognize as his, I kept walking. Right into him. My nose smashed directly into his back, the hit somewhat cushioned by his navy cashmere sweater. "Oops. Ouch. Sorry," I mumbled. But I wasn't too sorry because my scent memory recaptured our first Mardi Gras parade when you spilled your beer on my thigh and licked it off, and shrimp po-boys at the lakefront, and making supper after making love, and sleeping pressed into the crook of your arm.

"You okay?" He turned and reached out as if to grasp my hands, but I was already using both of them to massage my nose.

"This is my car . . . wait, I forgot you didn't know that," he said.

Since he sounded almost apologetic, I skipped the barbed wire response I had ready about ex-fiancés paying for BMWs instead of honeymoons.

Just as Levi opened the passenger door for me and impressed me with his throwback to politeness, my cynic elbowed its way to the tip of my brain. *Don't kid yourself. He didn't want you to open the door. You might have swung it open so hard that you'd crack the paint job on the red truck parked next to his.*

He slid into the driver's seat, and even my cynic grudgingly admitted he could one-up any actor in a car commercial. The man wore success well.

I rubbed my hand over the buttery leather, barely aware he'd already started the car. I fastened my seatbelt. "So, this is what it's like to sit in the lap of luxury."

"If you want, I can warm your seat," he said.

I was astonished and turned on simultaneously. "You move faster than the car. Are we back to that stage in our relationship so soon?"

He laughed. Almost a belly laugh. "I meant the seat warmer."

It was almost disappointing.

We decided talking at the bakery made the most sense since my car was parked there and we'd be less likely to be seen, if at all.

His story of buying the car filled the time and space between us, and it didn't require my rapt attention, which meant I could look out the window at the Christmas decorations. Homes dripping in lights, front doors draped with garlands, lawns displaying manger scenes or blow-up Santa's or wooden reindeer figures. In Deep South Louisiana, like Magnolia Hills, Christmas isn't sleigh bells jingling, Jack Frost nipping or Yuletide fires burning. We don't get to sing songs about wreaths on streetcars or eating pralines instead of sugar plums or Santa in a pirogue pulled by alligators. Levi and I used to joke that our ticket to fame and fortune would be writing Christmas songs with titles like, "Y'all Be Sure to Go to Your Mama n'Thems for Christmas, A Jazzy Christmas, Baby It's Barely Cold Outside and Eating Gumbo After Midnight Mass."

This year, how I felt about Christmas had nothing to do with geography. It was a "Blue Christmas," and I hoped it wouldn't get any bluer.

Chapter Five

✎

LEVI TURNED ON TO MAIN STREET, which had been decorated the week before with the traditional aluminum framed Christmas trees outlined with white twinkling lights and attached to tops of utility poles lining the street. "Seeing those driving in," he said and pointed to the trees, "made me really feel like I was home. Not just the knowing I'd reached Magnolia Hills, but realizing I was some place comfortable and familiar, you know?"

I did know. It was how I felt right then, seeing the profile of his face as he drove, how he sometime tapped his fingers on the steering wheel when he stopped at a red light, and how he slowed at Dead Man's Curve to glance at the perpetual cross planted there after one of our high school friends died going off the road. Of course, I didn't say any of that when he parked next to my car at the back entrance of the bakery. I nodded in reply, knowing whether he saw me or not, he already knew my answer.

"They're in here somewhere," I said digging through the black hole of my purse to find my keys.

"Why don't you—" Levi stopped when I glared at him as if he'd just eaten the last fried shrimp on my plate.

Smirking at the familiar exchange, my response flowed as easily as the wine had earlier. "Put them in the same place every time? Because the search and discovery are so much more exciting. You've asked me this question for years."

"Exactly," he said, a smile playing on his lips. He leaned against the building while he waited, his arms crossed and his lips looking entirely too kissable for my own damn good.

Before the throbbing in my heart propelled me to lead him back to the car and stretch him across the back seat and relive high school sexcapades all over again, I found the key. Seconds after I opened the door and flipped on the lights, the alarm started pinging. I entered the code. It didn't stop. "Crap." I dropped my purse on the floor. Tried again. Still pinged. In a few seconds, the damn thing would blare louder than police sirens leading a Mardi Gras parade. "Crap. Crap." *What the hell?*

Why wasn't the damn code working?

Out of the corner of my eye, I saw Levi attempting to appear unconcerned by reading the EEOC guidelines posted on my office wall. Then, seconds after the alarm repeatedly screeched, "Intruder Alert" to the background melody of howling whoop-whoop-whoop, it hit me. I'd been entering the code for our house, the one Levi and I shared.

By the time I entered the right code, my cell phone rang. "Hi, Holly, it's Nadine at the alarm company. Did Preston change the code on you?"

I rubbed my forehead as if I could get the stupid out. "No, just a brain cramp."

"Honey, you probably shouldn't be working that late anyway. You be careful."

"Thanks, Nadine. Tell Andrae hello for me."

"Will do, darling. Do the same for Levi, okay?"

What the hell?

I ended the call and shook my phone at Levi. "Did you tell Nadine Pruitt that you were in town?"

"What are you talking about? I haven't talked to anyone but you, Preston and your friends at the bar."

We looked at one another and, at the same time, said, "Preston."

Blessings and curses of small town life. Being

on a first name basis with the couple who own the alarm company, and using that company because it's owned by your partner's brother.

"Well, so much for flying under the radar," I said.

Levi shrugged. "I didn't tell Preston that my being here or wanting to see you was classified information." He looked around my office. "Going for the minimalist approach?"

"No, smart ass. We haven't even opened yet, so furnishing my office isn't high on my priority list." I grabbed two foldout chairs leaning against a white plastic table that served as my desk and handed him one. "Not much to offer," I said as I opened the mini-fridge in the corner. "Water, orange juice, or a bottled Starbucks Vanilla Frap." Magnolia Hills hadn't snagged a Starbucks store yet, but with commercial property ownership passing to the next generation, I was moving the possibility off my bucket list and onto my wish list.

"Water," he said. "You have any samples hanging around waiting to be taste tested?"

"Samples? Really?" I handed him a water bottle and opened one for myself. I stood, gaping, and all the thoughts pushing against the gate of my forced composure tumbled out. "Did you drive for hundreds of miles to hangout at an unopened bakery, drink water, and hope for cookies? Do you realize how incredibly annoying and nerve-wracking and frightening it is for you to appear out of nowhere after I haven't talked to you or seen you for months?" I stopped pacing and stood in front of Levi who'd been watching me with an expression as flat as the floor. My hands on my hips, I narrowed my eyes and told him, "If you're here to dispense bad news, then spit it out. Don't torture me. And, if that's not why you're here . . . well, let's stop screwing around with small talk."

"I don't know how you're ever going to be successful here if that's how you answer customers who ask for samples." He smiled—one of those slow, easy smiles drawn in wet sand—set his water on the corner of my desk and reached for my hands. "I missed this. Your adorable intensity—"

"Don't patronize me." I pulled my hands away before the surge of his touch took me places I wasn't ready to go. "And don't touch me." I rubbed my clammy palms on my jeans. "And don't look wounded because I said that."

Levi stood, placed his hands on my shoulders, and said, "Holly, look at me. I'm here because I've been miserable without you." He held my face in his hands, traced my lips with his thumbs. "I hated every morning I woke up without you, and every night I went to bed with my arms empty." He kissed my forehead, and I moved my hands over his as they cradled my face.

When he leaned over and brushed his lips against mine, soft and delicate, I felt like I was sixteen again, and feeling his mouth touch mine for the first time. I closed my eyes and lost myself in his tenderness. Felt my cheeks grow hot as the warmth of his breath traveled from my lips to my eyes. My own breath was shallow and uneven, anticipating the softness of his mouth.

"I love you," he whispered against my ear, and then he found my mouth again, teasing my lips open with his tongue and then we were Levi and Holly again, pressed against each other, my arms around his neck, his fingers moving through my hair, drawing my face closer until I can barely breathe or stand for the trying to satisfy our hunger for one another.

When his mouth moved to my neck, I said, "I love you, too. Does this mean you're coming home?"

Levi's fluttering kisses against my neck stopped, and he pressed his forehead against mine. "I'm not coming home to stay. I came to take you with me."

That was not at all what I expected or wanted to hear.

Chapter Six

❧

I BACKED OUT OF THE garage the next morning on my way to the bakery to find Momma standing at the edge of the driveway.

Beating my head against the steering wheel might have saved me the pain of getting out of the car to ask why she was outside, fully dressed, at 6:45 in the morning. But, the reality was, I'd be damned if I stopped. Damned if I didn't.

Black fabric had been draped over her dead camellia bush, so I prayed she wasn't biding her time, waiting for the magic stroke of seven o'clock or something before she walked across the street to raise holy hell at Beulah Grace's. Levi's car was there, and I couldn't face the two of them and my mother. Not after last night. My eyes were already red and puffy from crying. I didn't want to know how contorted my face could become from screaming.

"Good morning, Momma." I kissed her cheek and tasted Pond's Cold Cream on my lips. "I wondered where you'd disappeared to after I woke up this morning."

"I disappeared to right here to wait for Shorty Lemoine's bus." She looked at her watch. "Should be by in the next five minutes or so."

I had to take the bait because I had no idea of her pending lunatic plan. "Reliving your junior high days? Or is this new transportation for substitute teachers? If it's their new ride, it's actually not a bad idea because—"

"Did you see that fancy foreign car parked outside the Schwartz house? Wonder who that belongs to? You know, this country wouldn't be in so much trouble if more people bought American." Amazing. She looked like my mother, and she sounded like my father.

"I'm sure the person who owns it bought it from an American." The car's owner might be a traitor, but I left that part out. I pushed my sunglasses on my head. "You ignored my question."

She scanned my face. "What's wrong with you? Probably allergic to one of those fancy night treatments you're always buying. You're already pretty, so stop wasting your money on all that nonsense."

This conversation was a runaway train, and the last place I wanted to be was stranded on the tracks when Levi left his house. "Thanks for the compliment and the advice, but you still didn't tell me why you're out here. And if I don't get to the bakery soon, Preston's going to call out the National Guard." *Because I called him last night after Levi left me. Again.* "I'm pretty sure there must be some law in the state of Louisiana that private citizens can't board school buses. And I really don't want to be baking cakes with saws in them to bring to you in jail."

"Speaking of jail. . .that's why I'm waiting for Shorty. I want to know if she," Momma pointed at Beulah Grace's house, "can be arrested for killing my camellia bush," she said and looked so smug, I wouldn't have been surprised to see her pat her own back.

"Oh, dear God." I found my cell phone in my pocket and called Preston to tell him I was still alive, but I'd be late, and I'd explain when I got there. *Why didn't schools close earlier for Christmas so I wouldn't have to deal with this damn bus?* "Momma, you can't stop the school bus to ask Shorty such a ridiculous question just because he's the sheriff. Why don't you wait until his route's over and go see him at his office?"

She straightened her embroidered denim

34

blouse over her denim pants as soon as she spotted the bus stopping a block away. No mistaking those squealing brakes. Sounded like a hundred pigs in a sty all getting frisky at the same time.

I mentally made a quick list of things I wanted God to take care of in the next two minutes. *Don't let Beulah Grace or Levi walk out of their house. Give Mrs. Casnave next door a reason to go back in her house. Let Shorty not be driving the bus today. If he is, help Shorty not think my mother is like Mrs. Hightower who's so dense, she could throw herself on the ground and miss.*

"Momma, how about if I go with you to visit Shorty? I could bring him a few samples from the bakery." *Because Levi certainly didn't get any last night . . . in more ways than cookies.* "That might help your cause." Wait until Preston heard *this* reason for my needing to leave early today.

The bus rumbled its way toward us, a huge red and green tinseled wreath tied to its grill. I could tell the wheels in Momma's brain were turning, too.

"That's a good idea, Holly, but what am I supposed to tell him now? He's almost here, and I'm already standing on the curb like some Bourbon Street floozy."

I faked a coughing spasm so she wouldn't think I was doubled over with laughter. I was. In fact, on that one, I could have tripled over. "Since you're with your daughter, I doubt if he'll mistake you for a hooker," I said. I put my arm around her shoulders. "And don't worry. I'll handle this."

The two of us against the Schwartzs. My life was turning into a twenty-first century Hatfields and McCoys feud.

Chapter Seven

ARRIVING AT THE BAKERY, I couldn't wait to share my story of my morning with Momma with Preston. His array of reactions moved from, "Oh, no girl, tell me she did *not* say that," to "She said *what?*" to "Your Momma is cray-cray. I'm telling you, that woman is one sandwich shy of a picnic."

One of Preston's many endearing, and I hoped enduring, traits was his laughter. I had told him for years that we should make a YouTube video so hospitals and treatment centers could use it as part of their healing protocol. Every bone in his body was his funny bone. All six feet four inches of him participated in the response. His mahogany eyes flashed, then his mouth stretched into a broad smile that revealed a row of perfectly veneered and brightened teeth. His chest and stomach vibrated until there was an explosion of sound as if he was being endlessly tickled. He held his sides and pretended to writhe in the delicious pain of it all or bend over and slap the tops of his thighs with the palms of his hands, and later gasped for breath.

All in all, to experience Preston laughing was a performance well worth the price of a concert ticket, and anyone who heard him couldn't help but laugh themselves. It was a catharsis that brought people to happy tears. And happy tears were exactly what I needed.

Preston sat in my office, in the same chair as Levi the night before, wiping his eyes and recovering from our laughter binge. "Okay, now that I've heard all about your Momma, you need to fill me in on what happened between you and Mr. I Have a New BMW. Then, we need to get busy on our business. We should be busier than two moths in a mitten there's so much work to do.

"I know. Somewhere around here I have a 'to do' list of my 'to do' lists." I slumped in my chair behind my wobbling folding table desk and regretted not paying more attention to the "Putting Paperwork in Its Place: Creating the Paperless Work Space" webinar a few months ago. I took notes. Those notes were probably buried in one of the five stacks in front of me, but it would take me to longer to find the notes than re-watch the seminar.

I parted the papers on my desk to make room for our lunch of egg rolls and fried rice Preston brought from home. The man baked and cooked, and not just pedestrian red beans and rice. Crawfish and tasso chowder, black truffle and mushroom risotto, and sweet potato catfish. He loved to iron, he decorated, and he didn't hesitate to tell me when my clothes were frumpy. Some days he gave me reason to question why I was marrying a straight man.

I handed him the soy sesame sauce for the egg rolls. "Before I launch into this depressing drama between Levi and me, and keeping in mind that you are totally transparent, was his 'dropping by' really a surprise?"

"Yes and no," he said. "And let a man eat one bite of food before you get your answer."

I waited until he finished chewing. "It wasn't a two-part question. Explain."

"Yes, it was a surprise because I had no idea until he called me when he hit Baton Rouge. And, before you ask, he called me first to make sure you were here, as in Magnolia Hills here. And he didn't know if you might be, you know, busy."

I almost choked on my rice. "Busy? Define 'busy' would you?"

"I'm guessing he meant as in out with one of the many eligible bachelors in our fair town. Give the man some credit. He knows you're a catch, and he wasn't taking anything for granted."

"First, I have no clue if or where there's a stable of 'eligible bachelors.' Second, assuming such a thing exists, you're the only eligible bachelor I'd be interested in. And, third," I tossed my plate in the trash having lost my appetite to the conversation, "I'm still not sure if I'm insulted or flattered by him thinking that."

"Do you want to hear the rest of my answer or are we going to be writing more invitations to your pity party first?"

I rolled my eyes, which he took as his cue to continue. While I listened, I compiled the hills of papers on my desk into one mountain and sorted them into invoices, price lists, crap and more crap.

"I told him it was Girls' Night Out, but I was waiting for LamarAnn to call to let me know where y'all were going. I figured by the top he got to town, it was easier for him to stop here. So, that's the 'no' part. Now, your turn. I haven't heard that much sobbing since my friends found out Cher's Madison Square Garden concert got cancelled. I could only understand maybe every third word, so you might as well take it from the top."

"You know that cliché definition of insanity? The one about doing the same thing, expecting different results? Levi not only does the same thing, he does even worse than the same thing. He tells me he misses me, can't live without me, blablahblah, and I think the next thing he's going to tell me is that he's moving back. But no."

Not only is he staying in Houston, they're talking about another transfer as early as six months from now. And wait for it . . . to South Korea for God's sake. What the hell? Why would I move over seven thousand miles away when I don't want to move less than three hundred miles? And to South Korea?

Chapter Eight

⁓

BY THE TIME PRESTON AND I finished discussing everything that needed to happen before our Grand Opening, I thought I'd have to add a Prozac prescription to the list for him. His tendency for high drama was exacerbated by a phone call to the bakery from one frantic Millie Shoemaker, program chairperson for the Friends of the Library Book Bash. The Book Bash was their annual fundraiser and silent auction and, not only did it draw the Magnolia Hills elite, it attracted a few—as Mille called them—"highfalutin" people from New Orleans.

"Lord, Holly, that caterer just up and died on us, bless her heart. And I mean, died, as in we're going tomorrow to pay our respects before the funeral. Vicky was my second cousin on my daddy's side, and she's been doing our galas since forever. I guess sooner or later she was going to run

out of steam, so to speak. She made eighty-one just
two days ago. Anyway, darling, naturally her poor
husband's about as useful as a football bat right
now. But the night before Christmas Eve, we're
expecting at least one hundred fifty people, and
don't have one sweet thing to serve them."

I reassured Miss Millie that we'd come to her
rescue, and then reassured Preston that we could
pull it off.

"Do you want me to call your mother and tell
her that your happy ass needs to be here baking
and not taking her to sway the sheriff into a
conviction?"

"This won't take long. I promise. I already
called Shorty to give him the heads up, so he'll be
prepared when we get there," I said as I gathered
caramel brownies, cinnamon and apple fritters,
peach and pecan scones, and cake balls of
cheesecake, red velvet, carrot cake and German
chocolate. I set them inside one of our green and
yellow striped pastry boxes, sealing it with an
MHB label.

"If you're not back here in an hour, I am firing
myself," said Preston.

"Got it," I said. I didn't want to tell him that
it's hard to take a man wearing a pale yellow apron
imprinted with, "Don't judge me," seriously.

WHEN I HANDED Shorty the box of pastries, his eyes twinkled like a five-year-old who'd been told he could eat dessert before dinner. I'm certain that's exactly what happened because he worked over a brownie and one fritter while we talked.

Momma gave him a stack of our business cards. "There's more where these came from, so don't hold back giving them out. Maybe you could give some to your patrol men."

"Patrol people. Not all of them are men, and I'm not sure handing them a Mad Hatter's Bakery card with a ticket is a good marketing idea," I said. "And please don't ask him to hand them out in the jail."

"As if." Momma huffed and was close to pouting, so I dove into the reason we were there as though Shorty and I hadn't had a few laughs about it already.

"My mother thinks that—"

"No, honey, I *know*," she said and scooted to the front of her chair as if she was about to hold court on Shorty's desk.

I patted her shoulder and tried to nudge her back a bit. "Anyway . . . there have been a few situations between Beulah Grace and my mother over the past few months. So, when her camellia bush died, she had reason to believe," I stopped to make eye contact with Momma, "that she might have done something to kill her plant. Now, she wants to press charges, but I'm not sure about that as far as the law's concerned."

Shorty, God love him, took notes while I spoke, nodding at the appropriate times, and Momma nodded right along with him.

"And that's why Holly suggested we talk to you. I want to know what my rights are and if she can be arrested for assault or battery."

Assault on an unarmed plant?

Shorty continued his note-taking, which probably helped him to maintain his serious expression. Though he did have to cough behind his hand once or twice. A tactic I knew well.

"Mrs. Pressfield, do you have surveillance cameras outside your house? Or would any of your other neighbors possibly have seen Mrs. Schwartz on your property about the time you think this may have happened?"

"Oh, sweetie, call me Nancy Jane. And, no, we don't have cameras. That's why we live in Magnolia Hills, right? So we don't have to bother with all that nonsense. Now, my other neighbors. . ." Momma tapped the fingertips on both hands together, her eyes fixed somewhere over Shorty's head, her lips pursed. "It was so early . . ." she mused and rested her chin on her now still hands.

Shorty had just bit into the fritter when Momma plopped her hands in her lap and sighed. "For the life of me, I can't remember anyone who might have been out that morning. But if I do—"

"You call me as soon as you do. As for pressing charges, Louisiana does have a criminal mischief law which carries a sentence of up to six months in jail and a fine of up to five hundred dollars. But . . . without proof that Mrs. Schwartz is guilty of killing your camellia bush, I'm afraid there's not much else that can be done."

I shook my head, folded my hands in my lap and pinned Momma to her chair with my eyes. "You would send my ex-almost-mother-in-law to jail and want her fined than she was paying for our rehearsal dinner for your bush?"

"I might not be able to win the Christmas Garden of the Month, which means I could miss that trip to the annual convention," she said.

Shorty and I exchanged glances, and I played the trump card he and I had talked about when I called him earlier. I leaned over to Momma and put my hand on her knee. "You are underestimating yourself. Do really think you would be defeated by one camellia bush? And what happened to peace and goodwill? Look around here." I waved my arm Vanna White-like. "They're collecting for Toys for Tots, and people are wearing Santa hats and picking names of families off the Christmas tree to prepare meals for. Don't you think you can rise above this?"

Momma brushed something invisible to the naked eye from her black crepe pants, and I detected a faint blush rising from her neck. She stood and looked from me to Shorty and back again. "Don't think I don't know what the two of you are up to. You're trying to make me feel ashamed for being so angry at Beulah Grace." Momma clutched her purse in front of her stomach like a shield. "Sometimes people just need to learn a lesson, and that woman has pushed me one too many times."

Shorty nearly choked on what was left of his fritter. He looked like a deer caught in headlights.

And she wasn't finished. "Holly and I have to leave, but I'll be expecting a phone call from you on your progress."

Chapter Nine

ꜱ

THE DISTANCE BETWEEN MY HOUSE and the police station seemed shorter than the distance between Momma and me in the car.

I drove the two miles waiting for her to speak first. She didn't. She spent the two miles telling me about Lily and "the boys" not being able to be in Magnolia Hills until Christmas Eve because of her husband having to work at their restaurant.

Our silence the two miles home spoke for us.

When I pulled into the driveway, I saw the BMW that had still been parked across the street when I picked Momma up was now gone. Once again, a part of me left with it. I hadn't told my parents that Levi was in town. They may have already heard. And if they hadn't yet, they would. The timing was simply a question of what other spicy stories were traveling through town. Sometimes, even the Magnolia Hills Facebook page would have "prayer requests," news flashes under the guise of care and concern. Posts like, "Please keep the Wagner family in your prayers. Their son's back in rehab, and they may lose their house if Fanny's laid off because of her morning sickness."

Before Momma opened her passenger door, I said, "I think you're being stubborn about this. It's not Levi's mother's fault we're not engaged."

"Never once blamed her for that. There's a Garden Club meeting tomorrow, and the judging is Christmas Eve before noon. I have a lot of work to do, so I'm probably not going to be cooking supper. Already informed your daddy."

I nodded. "Thanks for letting me know." And before she could close the door, I said, "I love you anyway."

"I know," she replied.

I watched her unlock the front door. She looked defeated and sad instead of a staunch defender of her principles. I hadn't noticed earlier that her pants looked baggy, and her blouse, which tended to fit snugly over her hips, hung loosely. Had she been on a diet, and I didn't even notice her weight loss?

I sent Preston a text to let him know we finished earlier than expected, and I'd be there soon. Turning onto Azalea Drive, the street that led out of our neighborhood, I saw a now familiar, white BMW heading in the opposite direction.

Levi hadn't left.

I wasn't sure if my heart pounding was anxiety or relief.

I PARKED IN the front of the bakery when I spotted Preston hanging the temporary banner we ordered since our sign wasn't going to be delivered until after the first of the year.

"Did Levi stop by while I was gone?"

He glared down at me from the ladder. "Oh, hello partner. No, I don't need any help or thank yous or 'that looks very nice, Preston' because I am a marginalized gay black man working to please one itty bitty woman who only cares about herself."

I squinted, shielding my eyes with my hands to see him clearly. "So, does that mean he didn't?"

"Do you see what I'm holding in my hand? It's a hammer, and if I drop it from this distance it could cause damage to even your damn hard head." He nailed the last corner under the eave and climbed down.

"Come on, grouch. Let me give you one of those Duggar family pre-wedding sideways hugs," I said and held out my arms.

"Oh, but no. You deserve one bear hug from a

man who's been dripping sweat for at least an hour." He laughed and pretended to throw his arms around me, but he gave me time to escape, so I dashed inside.

Preston and I met in the Culinary Arts Program in high school. We both seriously considered dropping the class because nothing about frying, sautéing, roasting or broiling rocked our worlds. But when the class moved into desserts, we found our passion. At first we thought it might have been for one another, until we realized what really turned us on was fondant and buttercream icing and chocolate anything. We joked then about opening a business together, and years later, when we both found ourselves back in Magnolia Hills we resurrected the idea.

When Preston and I started discussing a bakery, our original plan was to have a home-based business. But, that required a home. I lived in a garage apartment in the historic district. Barbie's DreamHouse kitchen was about the same size as mine. Levi had a home, but we were dating then, not engaged. It was easier to ask him which side of the bed he wanted to sleep on than which side of his kitchen he'd be willing to give up. Preston had just moved back home from Austin after his partner of five years changed his mind and decided he wanted to adopt a child. They struggled for six months trying to make the relationship work, but as Preston explained to me later, "Compromise was impossible. You just can't have half a child."

Preston had a home, then two months into our planning, his sister's landlord decided to sell the house she and her husband rented. So, Preston, whose heart is about the size of Alaska, and who had a settlement from his former pediatric neurologist partner, moved the couple into his house, and he bought a smaller garden home.

So, when the "For Sale" sign went up on the Victorian house smack in the middle of Main Street, we decided it was destiny calling. Preston said it was Betty Crocker, Martha Stewart, and Carlo, the Cake Boss.

That afternoon, looking at the tens of thousands of dollars invested in equipment, supplies, packaging, advertising and inventory, and seeing "The Mad Hatter Presents Its Grand Opening" banner, for a minute . . . just one little minute . . . South Korea seemed appealing.

Chapter Ten

❧

"YOU KNOW THAT EXPRESSION ABOUT the cobbler's kids not having shoes?" I sat at one of the café tables putting Almond and Lemon Biscotti dipped in White Chocolate into green and yellow dotted cellphone bags.

Preston stopped mixing the batter for his Rosemary, Pear and Asiago Scones. "And?"

"Look out there and around here," I said, waving my hand. "What's wrong with this picture?"

"We don't have a poster advertising Barbra Streisand entertaining us at the opening?" He shook his head. "And it's a damn shame. I sent her agent an invite." Preston then stared at the ceiling, glanced at the walls, and shrugged. "Sister, if I don't get these scones in the oven soon, I'm going to start eating this loveliness"—he pointed to the mixing bowl—"with my bare hands, so just tell me."

"Christmas!" I carried the bagged biscotti to one of the display cases and arranged it in an oval wicker basket. "We bought Christmas-y ribbon and bags and bows to wrap the food, but we forgot a Christmas tree, decorations, and don't even have a wreath for our door."

"We don't have Hanukah menorah or Ramadan paper lanterns either." Preston slid the tray of scones into the oven. When he turned and saw my face, which if it looked like I felt, was not a pretty sight. "You need to relax. It's not as if we don't have a hotline to the diva decorators of the Hills."

"True . . . but, I'm not exactly at the top of the 'eager to please' list of either one of the two women who'd come to my rescue faster. By now, there are voodoo dolls hanging on the mantel of Levi's mother's house that look a lot like me and my mother. I expect to start twitching at any time. As for Nancy Jane, well, she's too preoccupied with pulling off the Best Christmas Garden in the universe to buzz over here to help."

"Don't Allee and Mia belong to the Garden Club? I've seen their homes, and I'm sure they inherited a decorator gene from someone," Preston said. "Don't buy into that myth that only gay men can pull off fabulous decorating." He laughed.

"You're right. They're more into the 'club'

than the 'garden' part, so I'm guessing they're not frantically flinging lights and fake snow all over their lawns." I sent them a text asking them to call me about a mission of mercy. They'd know that meant I needed help.

Preston washed his hands and picked up a clipboard in each hand. "Want me to start on pies or pound cakes?"

"Pound cakes." I carried a tray of hazelnut biscotti to the table. "Have you noticed anything different about my mother? Like has she said anything to you about going on a diet?" I sampled one of the broken biscotti. Perfect. Crisp with a dense texture and a whisper of hazelnut. Now if I only had a cup of hot coffee for dipping. . .

"Are you eating the inventory already? Because if you are, you could share." Preston assembled his ingredients for zucchini and walnut pound cakes, and ate one of the biscotti I brought him. He closed his eyes as he chewed. "Good work, Preston, if you have to say so yourself." He winked at me. "I haven't seen your Momma lately. You sound worried? Is she so skinny she can't see her shadow?"

I cut lengths of gold organza ribbons for the bags and started assembling again. "No. She did say she'd wanted to lose weight for the wedding. Maybe she's at that point where it's showing," I said, but the concern lingered.

Christmas music streamed from Preston's iPhone while they worked. Sometimes they lip synced along with Bruno Mars' "White Christmas," Cee Lo Green's "All I Want for Christmas," and Preston went into full vocals along with Springsteen's "Santa Claus is Coming to Town." But when I heard Elvis Presley's "Blue Christmas," the lyrics and the melody crashed through the flimsy wall that separated my past from my present. My eyes and nose started stinging, my lips twitched, and my hands trembled.

I don't know if the crinkling cellphone or my wet sniffles alerted Preston, but the song switched to __and a handful of tissues materialized in front of me. Preston made soft circles on my back with one hand and patted my shoulder with the other. "I know. I know. When you think you've protected yourself, taken all those years together and shoved them in a vault, the pain zeroes in like a stealth missile. Before you know it, you're picking fragments of memories from places in your body you didn't know existed."

Preston sat in a chair across from mine, moved the biscotti to the side, and held my hands in his. "We think love is enough, and sometimes it is, sometimes not. But you have to decide if you're going to follow your heart or your head. We can have all we want, just maybe not at the same time." He leaned across the table and hugged me. "How about us belting out "Let It Go" from *Frozen* while we finish what we started here, and then heading to the Christmas store for some retail therapy?"

I wiped my cheeks and eyes, blew my nose, and nodded.

Preston took his scones out of the oven, and put in the pound cakes. "Honey, when the going gets tough, the tough go shopping. Trust me, I have a closet of price-tagged crap to prove it."

Chapter Eleven

❧

PRESTON AND I WERE NEXT in line to check out at The Christmas Palace when Shorty's phone number popped up on my cell phone. Any other time in my life, the sheriff calling would suck the breath out of my body. This afternoon, I considered letting the call go to voicemail until I had the emotional energy to hear the latest installation of the Great Camellia Bush saga of Magnolia Hills.

But, just in case I'd live the rest of my life regretting I missed the call informing me that someone I loved hovered between life and death, I answered. "Hey, one minute, I'm stepping outside." I mouthed Shorty's name to Preston, handed him the bakery credit card, and walked out of the store. Rain fell in misty sheets, and the temperature had dropped while we'd been shopping. *Great. One more delay in our Fa-La-La-*

La-La decorating.

"Hi, Shorty. You already talked to Beulah Grace?"

"You might could say that," he said.

That answer didn't trumpet good news was about to follow. I turned and waved at Preston who'd reached the cashier and was still unloading our cart. He made a "thumbs up" sign. I shook my head. He made a face like he'd just found half a worm in his apple.

My hand over my eyes as if it could shield me from the image of doom I anticipated appearing in my mind, I asked the question I dreaded. "What happened now?"

"Everybody is fine. So, don't worry about that. But . . . I got your mother and Mrs. Schwartz in my office right now—"

"What the hell . . ." I must have been louder than I realized because a woman leaving the store with a little boy sitting in the basket, slapped her hand on her hip, and glared at me. "There's a child here," she said, her reprimand as tight as her lumpy leggings.

I rolled my eyes and faced the other direction. "Sorry, Shorty. I'm not upset with you. Go ahead and explain." I pinched the bridge of my nose and waited.

"The Garden Club meeting was at Mrs. Boudreaux's house today, and from what I'm heard—because it was mostly all over by the time they called me—your mother and Mrs. Schwartz argued over how many poinsettias to buy for the church and who should host the annual Christmas party. I'm still not sure how it all started, but your mother pulled all the petals and leaves off the poinsettias Mrs. Schwartz brought to the meeting to give Mrs. Boudreaux. Then Mrs. Schwartz grabbed all the fruitcake slices your mother brought, crumbled them and tried to dump them on your mother's head. According to Mrs. Boudreaux and some of the other members, there was a whole lot of shrieking and accusing and—as they called it—'unnecessary language not meant for ladies to hear.' "

Preston steered the basket in my direction and pointed to his car. I nodded and followed him, half-listening to Shorty, and half wondering how I could enter a Witness Protection Program. I helped Preston unload the bags since my part of the conversation was limited to, "Uh huh, Oh, crap, and I'm going to enter a convent."

By the time Preston slid behind the wheel, I'd finished talking to Shorty. I rubbed my temples and wished I had ruby slippers to click together three times, but I'd need to re-route them because home was not where I wanted them to take me.

"Where we going, Miss Daisy?" Preston started the car.

"To the police station to bust out two delinquent mothers," I said.

Before he left the parking lot, I tapped his arm. "Wait. Pull over. I have an idea." I called Shorty. "How soon do I need to get there?"

He laughed. "Take your time. I can move them to an empty office until you get here."

I looked at Preston. "On second thought. Let's go to lunch first. My treat," I said.

WHILE WE WERE eating at Casa Garcia, Allee sent me a text that she and Mia would stop by the bakery tomorrow so we could discuss what I needed them to do. "The elves will arrive tomorrow to talk about Christmas decorating," I told Preston.

"Great. I'll order some flan since I may not have to haul my butt up that ladder. At the rate I'm going, it would take two trips."

We finished lunch and arrived at the police station about an hour later. Shorty came out to meet us, and we followed him to his office.

"I think they're both fit to be tied," Shorty said and grinned. "They begged me to not call their husbands. I think they thought their kids would be here in a heartbeat to pick them up."

"Is Levi coming too?"

"His mother asked me not to contact him. She said he was driving to Houston, and she didn't want to upset him while he was traveling."

"So . . . Beulah Grace is leaving with us?" Levi left town without even so much as a text message that he was leaving, and I'm stuck with his mother. So much for he loves me, he misses me, and can't live without me. I thought about what Preston told me earlier about love sometimes not being enough to bridge the gap. He couldn't compromise with half a child, and Levi and I couldn't compromise with half the distance.

This nightmare was getting worse, not better.

"She wanted to take a taxi home, but I told her I wasn't releasing her to anyone but her son or you. No telling what would happen if she didn't have adult supervision while no one was at your house."

"Oh, this is better than watching Real House-wives of any city any day," said Preston. He laughed. "There's a reality show right here, just waiting to happen. Real Housewives of Magnolia Hills. Can you imagine?"

"You're scaring me because I know that look. It means you're a phone call away from trying to make it happen." I had to smile myself because an entire cast of characters had already assembled themselves in this city, and my mind was already rolling the credits. I eyed Preston. "Don't you dare."

"Now, there is a bit of information I need to tell you that I've already told the ladies." Shorty stood and opened his office door. "Mrs. Boudreaux might want them to pay for damages. I think a crystal vase might have broken, but I'm waiting for her to let me know."

"That money is definitely coming out of their allowances," I told Preston. "Now, where are these thugs?"

Chapter Twelve

⁂

PRESTON AND I WERE ON our way to drop off the two mommies dearest sitting behind us after, much to their humiliation, Shorty released them into our custody. "Y'all stay out of trouble because next time, I'll have to call your husbands. And, ladies, keep in mind that the manger didn't need to be decorated for it to be beautiful." He shook each of their hands and wished them a peaceful Merry Christmas. Walking past Shorty, who was a haircut away from being shorter than Preston, the two women looked like third graders leaving the principal's office.

They mashed their bodies against their respective doors in the back seat, and they each turned their faces to their windows. If they'd re-installed their senses of humors just a tad, I might have drawn an imaginary line on the seat between them with my finger and forbid them to say, "She's touching me." But, of course, not enough time had passed yet for them to find even ten seconds of funny in what happened this afternoon. Magnolia Hills could be a forgiving town, but forgetful? Not so much. Ed and Susie Palmer's daughter married a man from Rhode Island. Some people ask if she and that Yankee are still married. And that was over five years ago. Though they couldn't remember his name, they never forgot that he was from "up North somewhere."

The town's reaction would be either feast or famine. They'd get the silent treatment or their phones would be ringing every five minutes. The best they could hope for was being the first ones to explain what happened to their husbands. And both women lived in Magnolia Hills long enough to know they should have already called them.

Preston and I were discussing whether would should have a real or an artificial tree for the bakery when a ring tone I hadn't heard in months interrupted us. I showed Preston the caller ID. Levi.

"Answer it," he said softly.

I'd barely said, "Hello," when Levi asked in a voice moving over the speed limit, "Have you seen my mother? I've been calling for hours, and her phone keeps going to voicemail, and I'm worried. My dad's on a business trip to Chicago, so I didn't want to call him and ask. I thought you could tell me if her car was there or if you'd seen her. She mentioned something about a meeting this morning—"

"I know exactly where she is. And no reason to worry. Everyone is"—I surveyed the car. Preston, great. The backseat twins? Morose—I picked the average, fine. "We're all fine."

In fact, she and my mother are sitting right behind me in the back seat of Preston's car, and we're taking them home."

A long silence.

"I don't understand," he said.

"You will. Hold on." I handed my cell phone to Beulah Grace. "Levi wants to talk to you."

She shook her head, then turned to the window again.

"Mrs. Schwartz, Levi wants to talk to you," I said, my arm stretched over the seat holding the cell phone out to her. She didn't respond, and Preston was already turning into our neighborhood. After a futile second attempt to give the phone to Beulah Grace, I turned around in the seat, put the phone back up to my ear and relayed the news to Levi. "She, um, doesn't want to talk. But we're about two minutes from her house. Maybe you can call her."

"What the hell is going on, Holly? Can you

please tell me what this is about?"

"It's not life-threatening or dangerous, but she really needs to tell you herself . . ." I said, raising my voice to be certain Beulah Grace heard me.

"Tell her I'll be home in twenty minutes and for her to please not go anywhere until I get there."

Preston pulled into her driveway, and as I relayed Levi's message to his mother who looked as confused as I felt, it suddenly dawned on me that if Levi was twenty minutes away he either left really late to head to Houston or he hadn't left at all.

Beulah Grace paused, her hand on the door release, listening to the conversation.

"You're not on your way to Houston?"

"No. Long story . . . I have to take this call coming in. I'll be there soon."

I slipped my phone into my purse and gave Beulah Grace the last piece of information I knew. "Levi said he didn't go to Houston, but he didn't explain. I'm sure he'll tell you when you see him."

She started to close the car door, then she stopped and leaned in toward Preston and me. "Thank you," she said, her voice as flat as her sidewalk. She didn't look at my mother, whose head hadn't turned since she sat in the car. Beulah Grace opened her front door and didn't look back.

"Momma, do you want us to drop you off now? You can take a ride back to the bakery with us, and I can get my car and drive you home, if you'd rather do that instead."

No answer.

Preston turned around and with his honeyed voice said, "Miss Nancy Jane, I'm sure this has been a trying time for you. Now you're gonna have to pick yourself up, dust yourself off, and start over again. Nothing you don't already know living in this town all your life."

Her forehead against the window, Momma's fingers twisted her purse handles like knitting needles. Her veins roped through the tops of her hands like thick blue twine. She was twice my age, which tended to surprise people when they first met her, and who never suspected she had a daughter in her 30s. But pressed against the car door, pale and defeated, she looked every one of her sixty-four years.

Momma tended to tilt on the wrong side of crazy, so some things never surprised us. Like the year she made Lily and I each go through the grocery checkout line with her three times because turkeys were on sale, but the limit was one per customer. We came home with nine turkeys and a new freezer to put them all in because they clearly were not going to fit in our side by side.

My father tried to explain to her that saving ten dollars a turkey cost over four hundred dollars because of buying the freezer. "Nancy Jane, that's the kind of accounting the government operates on, and it's why they're taxing the hell out of us."

We had turkey for dinner the very next night because Momma read they'd be good frozen for only two years. "So, we have to eat four and a half turkeys a year to make sure they don't go to waste."

My father had a better idea. The week before Thanksgiving that year, he, Lily and I delivered seven turkeys to City Hall for the dinner they prepared for the homeless every year. On the way home, he told us if he could make each turkey worth fifty-seven dollars, the tax deduction would offset the cost of the freezer. "Of course, they don't sell for that much. But, you know, I think that's exactly how they'd do it in those government offices." Lily and I smiled because the idea seemed to make him happy. I was too young then to ask how he handled his taxes for that year, but now I'm glad I don't know.

I've learned there are things in life we're far better off not knowing. But what was sucking the life out of Momma and amping up her crazy was not one of those things.

Chapter Thirteen

"YOU'RE RIGHT ABOUT YOUR MOTHER. She has lost weight," said Preston as he watched Momma walk into her house. "But it's not so much the weight loss that concerns me. It's that she doesn't talk about it. Even if they don't come out and say how many pounds they've lost, women talk about how their clothes don't fit or they start buying clothes that show off they're not spread out like a cold supper anymore."

"And my father hasn't mentioned it, either. When we were in high school, she lost about thirty pounds. He started coming home with little pink bags from Victoria's Secret, grabbing her butt and telling her how sexy she looked. Lily and I slept with earphones because we didn't want to hear so much as a squeak coming from their bedroom. I still wear my earphones when I'm there."

"Call her tomorrow and invite her to lunch.

She needs you right now. And you need to be honest with her. Tell her you're concerned. She needs to hear that." Preston backed into the parking lot, and when we met at the trunk, I threw my arms around his waist and thanked him for being my constant when everything else seemed to be unpredictable. Preston assured me that everything would work out the way it was supposed to and reminded me I can't worry about those things out of my control. With all the chaos, I hadn't even realized that I needed that moment of human connection.

As we cleared the trunk of boxes and bags, I watched as Preston walked in front of me and thought about my gratefulness for those friends who become so entwined in your life that they started to feel more like family.

The trunk was empty, but our office was stuffed. I cleared a path through the clutter to be able to get to my desk. "Another lesson learned to add to not shopping for food on an empty stomach," I said as Preston handed me the receipts. "Don't buy Christmas decorations without a budget, especially when you're shopping with a friend who thinks the road to happiness is paved with glittery things, miles of mesh ribbon, and antique ornaments."

"You have wounded me. That is so not true."

Preston folded his hands over his heart. "The road to happiness is paved with Prada, Barbra Streisand, and Botox." He reached for his cell phone. "That was brilliant. I'm Tweeting it right now before it's lost forever in my brain. I should start a blog to post all of these illuminating thoughts. I could call them 'Prestonians," he said. "Maybe I could link it to our bakery website—"

"Stop." I held up my hand, then handed him one of the clipboards on my desk. "No linking. Just baking."

He glanced at the list. "Moving on to pies?" He slipped his apron on. "You're such a task master."

"I bet you say that to all your partners," I said as I tied on my own apron to start batches of brownies.

He looked up from the clipboard and grinned. "Oh, yes, and that's only the beginning."

I was taking my second batch of caramel and cream cheese brownies out of the oven when my father sent a text that he and Momma were leaving soon to have dinner in New Orleans, then they were going to see the Christmas lights in City Park.

"Good for him," said Preston after I'd read him the text. "He's getting her out of Magnolia Hills for the night."

"Too bad he can't get her out a little long-er. . .like a week."

A minute or so later, Preston stopped rolling out pie dough and asked me to send my father a text. "Tell him not to leave until I talk to him. Just five, maybe ten minutes."

"But—"

He held his hand up like I had earlier. "It's my turn to be the task master now. See how this works?" He scrolled through his phone. "I'm going to make a call while you send that text," he said and walked toward the rear of the bakery.

Within minutes he was back. "Give me your dad's number, and just listen so I won't have to repeat myself."

Preston told my father that the manager of The Roosevelt Hotel, a friend of his, was holding a room for him and Nancy Jane for the night. "Surprise her. No, you don't need to pack a suitcase. Just bring two toothbrushes. Sure. You're welcome. Have fun." He ended the call and smiled. "Your dad's excited. He said he'll buy two new toothbrushes and leave the used ones home. They need to get out more often."

"You are one of the kindest, most generous and—"

"Best dressed . . . don't forget . . ."

"Don't ruin this moment. I'm serious." I

hugged him again, and I didn't care that the pastry dough and cinnamon on his apron dusted my cheek. "Thank you, thank you, thank you," I said.

"My, my, my, we are huggy today," Preston said. "And you're welcome. The Beatles were right. We all need a little help from our friends to get by."

Chapter Fourteen

I DISCOVERED THE SECRET TO how to stop eating brownies. Bake fifteen dozen of them, and you'll start craving celery sticks. Maybe not craving, maybe not celery, but the notion of eating a brownie will seem like you're taking work home with you.

"I can't lift one more tray, bag one more item or read one more recipe. I'm hungry. I'm tired. I'm done for the day." I looked outside. "Night. Make that done for the night."

"I'm done with your whining." Preston turned off the oven. "Remember . . . you're the princess who told the library lady, 'No problem. Of course we can cater your ta-ta gala at the last minute, just days after our grand opening.' Did you quote her a price? Ask what their budget was for food?"

"Not really."

"You need to call her tomorrow before this

project ends up as charity work," he said. "Let's go home. We're both tired, and I'll go from snippy to all-out bitchy faster than little Lindsey Lohan gets pulled over if I don't get some rest.

We cleaned up, looked over what still needed to get finished, and decided to meet at six the next morning.

My cell phone vibrated in my pocket as I was walking to my car, and thinking it might be one of my parents, I answered without checking the number. It was Levi asking if I had plans for the night.

I sat in my car, and reclined my seat all the way back until I was staring at the roof. I loved the roof. It never needed cleaning. "Yes. A warm shower, hot food, and cool sheets. Exactly in that order." *And you're welcome to join me on one, two or all three.*

"Sounds like one of our typical nights. Is that an invitation?"

Damn. Did I say that aloud or was he reading my mind? I recognized that tone in his voice, how it wrapped itself around me like being cocooned in silk. My body had one answer, and my brain another. *When in doubt, misdirect.* "Is that why you called?"

"You're doing that thing again, . . . you're asking another question to avoid answering," he said.

I pictured the slow upward curve of his lips as he smiled, his eyes shining with the promise of his touch, and a tidal wave of longing threatened my defenses of logic and reason. I missed these verbal volleyball games with Levi when he moved to Houston, and we didn't speak to one another. Now, our conversation was familiar and comfortable, like knowing July would always follow June.

"My answer is maybe. Possibly. I don't know. It depends."

"A woman of conviction. I love that about you," he said and laughed.

He said "love," not "loved?" Levi seemed to be enjoying the easy banter between us. I, on the other hand, was tired, hungry and anxious. "Seriously, why did you call?"

"I wanted to talk to you about my mother. Our mothers. And if there's any way to repair this wreckage. I need to leave early tomorrow morning, so I thought us talking in person would be easier."

Leaving. Every time he said that, it felt like a paper cut. I've never heard anyone say, "Be careful with that paper, it might cut you." So, you're doing whatever it is you're doing with your paper, then . . . *whoosh* . . . swift, unexpected. Draws blood almost every time.

"I'm still sitting in my car in the bakery parking lot. I should be home in ten or fifteen minutes."

"Great. And I already picked up what we're having for dinner. I'll grill steaks and asparagus and we'll share a carton of Ben & Jerry's Coffee Toffee Bar Crunch." We used to joke that we were in a serious relationship with Ben & Jerry's, like Facebook status serious. Maybe it was a ménage à trois. Whatever it was, it was intense, passionate, and sticky. Very sticky.

"Thanks, I really didn't want. . .wait a minute, you already had everything before you called me?" I think I spit into my phone when I asked him, "You *expected* me to say, "Yes"?

"Nooooo," he said. "I hoped you would."

I opened the door still not having showered, which meant blotches of various color and textures adorned my jeans and my once spiffy blouse. Even wearing an apron, I leave almost every day with something on my clothes. "Make yourself at home," I waved him in to a house he knew almost as well as his own.

I followed him as he carried the grocery bags and a bottle of red wine to the kitchen. "No sneaking bites before dinner," he said and Ben & Jerry went into the freezer.

He left the steaks and asparagus on the island and looked around the family room. My parents' house was built to be so open, I was surprised they had bedroom doors.

"Not much has changed," he said shoving his hands in the pockets of his jeans, which fit him in all the right places.

If you don't count our missing engagement picture framed with our Save the Date announcement. Guess that counts as not much. "It's been less than four months. Momma redecorates every twenty-five years. My children will live to see the day."

He moved his head like he was watching a tennis match at Wimbledon. "Where are your parents?"

"Gone for the night. They left me all alone," I said. "Must have forgotten to mention that," I said in my feigned innocent voice.

He turned around and gave me that look. *That* look.

"I haven't showered yet," I said, knowing he would hear the invitation in my voice.

He did.

Chapter Fifteen

WHAT I LEARNED ABOUT SEX during Levi's absence:

1. skinny jeans should be labeled, "Not intended for those who will be engaging in quickies."
2. I missed it

Sultry seduction scenarios I sometimes allowed myself to envision, involving exquisitely prolonged unbuttoning and unzipping and any other undoing . . . Gone. When Levi looked at me with what I called his "bedroom eyes," the rest of the world fell away, whirled around us, waiting to reassemble itself and get on with the business and busyness of life. I stopped trying to explain when I'd hear one version or another of, "It means he wants sex. We get it." Because it truly was never about sex. Sex was never the ante; it was the payoff. Desire, passion, longing. Absolutely. But in that one moment, that one suspended beautiful moment, he sees past this shell of a body and captures my essence. I felt safe, protected, and filled with joy.

"I don't have the paperwork to prove it, but I think we just broke our own personal best in the fully clothed to naked event," I said and grabbed an armful of towels from the linen closet.

Levi took them from me and draped them over the towel bars. I closed the door and, as I stood there, drinking in his body, he moved closer to me.

"Not fair," I said leaning against the door, my bra and panties somewhere down the hall. I ran my finger inside the waist of his boxers. "Is the water ready because I'll be forced to remove these before we shower."

He smiled and reached for my hands. "Waiting for the water to get hot. I thought I'd give us time to do the same." He kissed the back of each hand, then turned them so he could kiss each palm. All the while, his eyes never left my face. Just those simple, tender kisses made me catch my breath.

"Stand back. I want to look at you. It's been too long . . ." He traced my face from one cheekbone to the other, pausing at my lips and outlining them with his thumbs as he cradled my face in his hands. "You are beautiful," he said, his own breath catching as he spoke. Then his eyes were his hands as they traveled down my body and up again. "Only this time, his hands traveled down the slope of my shoulders to my breasts, his fingers like feathers against my skin.

When his hands reached the curve of my hips, I covered them with my own. "I've missed this. I've missed you. I don't want you to leave." I didn't try to stop the tears. But I didn't need to. Levi drew me to him and his lips met mine. His fingers were wound in my hair as his mouth pressed against mine, familiar, but with an intensity born from hunger.

Steam billowed from the shower and surrounded us. I pulled away from Levi's lips long enough to lower his boxers down his muscular legs and, when they met the floor, he stepped out of them, grabbed my hand and led me to the shower. As he opened the shower door, my body shivered in anticipation of what would happen. I stepped into the shower and under the hot spray, and when I pulled my head back from under the water and opened my eyes, Levi stood in front of me, watching.

With only inches standing between us, we reacquainted ourselves with the other, with touches and kisses of anticipation and longing. The water was already turning cold when we lathered our bodies with soap, rinsed and got out of the shower.

Levi wrapped a towel around his waist and turned to wrap a towel around me. As I tucked in the corner of the towel above my breasts, Levi wrapped his arms around my waist, and picked me up carried me to bed. Opening my towel, his eyes traveled the length of my body as if he was seeing it for the first time. When his towel fell to the floor, I pulled him on top of me, feeling the bed dip with the weight of our bodies, looked directly into his beautiful eyes and told him to make love to me. Smiling, Levi, looked down at me and did just that. Twice.

Later, after Levi retrieved the bottle of wine and two glasses from the kitchen, we crunched pillows behind our backs, and leaned against the headboard. For a while, we simply soaked in the quiet and the surprising intensity of having reconnected. Not just physically, but emotionally.

"I love you, Holly. I want to make this work. And I understand that you've invested time and money in this bakery. I'm asking you to walk away from something you haven't started yet. But what if this transfer came through after we were married? Would you divorce me?"

"I've been asking myself that question almost every night since you left. When you first told me about the transfer, I really thought that if I refused to go, you would too. The closer the date came for you to go, the more we'd done at the bakery. So, when you wouldn't stay, and I wouldn't leave, I thought maybe that's a red flag, that you were always going to think what you did was more important than what I did. The last fight we had before you left, you told me that I'd rather have a bakery than a marriage.

"That was a sucker punch. I'm sure there would have been a nicer way to say that."

"No, it was exactly what I needed to hear because, then—mostly because I was so mad—you were right. I'd convinced myself that you didn't respect or value my work. Now, that I'm a little less angry," I leaned over and kissed his forehead, "I realize I wasn't respecting or valuing your work. I love this town. I always thought I'd raise my children here. Grow old here. A transfer was never on my radar, you know?"

He finished his wine and set his empty glass on the nightstand. "Mine, either. And I feel the same way about Magnolia Hills that you do, but if we were going to be married, I needed a job. You're not drawing a salary from the bakery yet, and I know you and Preston talked about doing that after the Grand Opening. But, we didn't know for sure. Even if you did start bringing home some money, there'd be times when we'd have to roll it back in. I never wanted you to give up the bakery for me. You'd always resent me. You have to decide if it's the life you want after I leave."

"But what about Preston? I agreed to be his partner. He's counting on me to be there."

"I understand exactly how he feels," said Levi.

"Oh, my God," I gasped. "I wanted to stay in Magnolia Hills because I agreed to be Preston's business partner. And you asked me to leave because I'd committed to being your partner in marriage, in life. You were counting on me too." I laid in bed and slapped my pillow over my head. "How could I not have seen that?"

"You weren't ready. But, now that you have, what are you going to do?"

"I know this for sure. That bakery might make me scream, but never in the way you did." I reached my arms around his neck. "I want to be your partner forever. We'll talk to Preston together. We'll make this work."

"Then, we're going to pick a date so I can finally see you in that amazing white dress I kept hearing about."

And then, he kissed me until I was breathless.

Chapter Sixteen

∽

LEVI AND I HAD JUST stepped out of our second shower when the doorbell lost its mind.

"Either some wire's tripped up or someone with a doorbell fetish is here. And I'm not expecting anyone, and I doubt you are," I said. I wrapped a towel around my wet hair and pulled on Momma's lovely robe I found in the bathroom closet. "I'm going up front to check out this damn Big Ben doorbell noise." Before I left, I watched Levi slip on his jeans because, really, who wouldn't want to watch?

"I'll start the steaks. You want yours rare, right?"

"Just like my men. Make that man."

Halfway down the hall, the doorbell noise blessedly stopped. I hadn't reached the guest room to find my clothes when a persistent knocking came from the back door.

There stood Beulah Grace pounding the window of the back door with her clenched hand. Good Lord, is this woman ticked off that Levi's here?

And, in perfect synchronicity, Levi walked into the den with, "I got your rare meat right here," at the same time I opened the door to let in his mother.

Kudos to her because if she heard her son, she didn't act as if she did. She planted her hands on her hips, glared between the two of us, and belted out, "If you two have been together for the last hour, one of you couldn't have answered your damn cell phone? I've been calling every ten minutes."

As usual, I had no clue in what mysterious place my cell phone might show up. It was like the Christmas Elf. It could be anywhere. And wherever Levi's phone might have been, we clearly were not paying attention to it.

Levi and I looked at one another, then at her. "So, why have you been so determined to get in touch with us?"

"Because Holly's daddy got tired of trying. Nancy Jane passed out when they were checking in at The Roosevelt Hotel."

Momma had been admitted at Tulane Medical Center in New Orleans. My father said the admitting doctor wanted to run some tests before they sent her home, otherwise; she was fine. "You know your Momma. She told me spending the night in the ER wasn't what she had in mind for a romantic night together. I told her I owe her one." He sounded tired, but not anxious, which made the one hour drive there a bit less frantic both for me and for Levi who drove. Daddy said he'd already talked to Lily, but he told her there wasn't any need for her to come in town early, especially because they weren't even there.

Beulah Grace told us to call her with updates, as did Preston who said he'd call the Girls' Night Out gang for me. "I know you've been worried about your Momma, so maybe this is a good thing because you weren't going to have much luck trying to get her in front of a doctor. Please tell her I'm going to have a little chat with God today about her, and that I think this is a drastic approach to getting out of cooking Christmas dinner."

I didn't tell Preston that I'd already called LamarAnn, told her what had happened, and asked if she, her sister and Mia could find time to help Preston today. "Our office is full of Christmas decorations, plus he's trying to get ready for the Grand Opening and the Library function," I said. "And you know he is too damn stubborn to ask anyone."

"Look, you relax about that Grand Opening. By tomorrow, your Momma being in the hospital will be conversation at most all of Magnolia Hills' dinner tables. So, people will understand if you and Preston postpone it," she said. "We'll slap up enough Christmas decorations so your customers won't think you're heathens or Santa-haters. But that Library gala's important because that could be referrals in the future. I'll tell him—no, what am I thinking—I'll *suggest* we work on the refreshments for that. Just like every man. You have to make them think it's their idea."

After Levi laughed, LamarAnn went silent for a moment. "You still there?" I asked.

"Yes. I forgot we were on the damn Bluetooth. Hi, Levi. You take good care of our girl."

"I already did," he said.

I turned fifty shades of red, and Levi just smiled at me and just shook his head.

"Levi, really. That's just too much information for me to handle by myself and without a glass of wine in my hand," said LamarAnn, an exaggerated sigh followed. "Guess you'll eventually fill us in, Holly, without the gritty details, how Levi *happened* to be around to take you to New Orleans."

"Both of us might be doing that," said Levi.

He smiled, and I reached over and squeezed his hand. "In the meantime, thanks for all you're doing."

"Oh, honey, our services come at a cost. We'll have a running tab in your name at The Whine Bar," she said.

"Fair enough," Levi answered.

I didn't want to borrow trouble, so I didn't tell Levi that what I did from this day on would largely depend on what the doctors said about Momma. I wasn't as sure as I wanted to be that everything was fine.

Chapter Seventeen

W HEN WE MET MY FATHER in the waiting room, he folded Levi into one of those man hugs and it touched me to witness how much he was missed.

"Have you had anything to eat, Hamilton?"

"Found some cheese crackers in one of the vending machines earlier. I'm not all that hungry. Mostly need that bed over at The Roosevelt," he said, his exhaustion evident in his weary eyes and the dark circles around them.

"Daddy, what are the doctors saying? And don't try to whiz past the hard stuff, okay? Just tell me," I said.

He explained that it wasn't just that Momma fainted that concerned the doctors. I told them about her losing weight, because—you know your Momma—she's damn self-sufficient and prideful."

"I think it's genetic," Levi told my father.

"Yep, I suspected that." Daddy smiled and nodded. He lowered his voice as if he suspected Momma could hear him, "I also mentioned how she just didn't seem to be herself lately. Getting all riled about that bush of hers, that foolishness at the club meeting. That's just not like your mother."

"No, it's more like *my* mother," said Levi. Daddy and I didn't disagree.

"So, that's what all those other tests are about. And the doctors have talked to both of us, so she knows, and she asks a lot of questions." He shook his head. "A lot. She's already asked me for a pen and paper to take notes."

"Why didn't you tell me that when I called? We could've picked that up along with something for you to eat other than hospital food," I said.

"She's probably going to be leaving here tomorrow. I didn't think she needed to start a diary or take doctor notes."

Levi and I glanced at one another hearing the edge in my father's voice. I hoped I wouldn't have to lead him out of the land of denial before this was all over.

My hand was on the door to Momma's room, and my insides were churning. I wasn't sure which version of her I was about to see. The last time we were together, she wasn't at her best, having just left Shorty's after she and Beulah Grace disturbed the peace of the garden club meeting.

I tapped as I slowly opened the door. "It's Holly, Momma." She was sitting up, remote control in hand, waving it at the television like it was a wand.

"Why are these damn things so complicated? Over four hundred channels, and I can't figure out how to get to one of them. Useless thing." She tossed it on the bed.

I bent over the bed rails and hugged her, holding on a little longer than usual. "I love you, Momma," I told her before I let her go. She smelled like rubbing alcohol and a bit of Pine-Sol. I smoothed her hair on the sides where it was all cattywampus, probably from being moved after she fainted.

"You didn't drive here alone, did you? It's not good to be gallivanting around here after dark."

"No. Levi drove me. We were . . . he came over to the house to grill steaks . . . it's long story."

"Seems like," she said and nodded, a grin on the way to a smile. "So, where is he?"

"He wasn't sure if you'd be comfortable with him just walking in. He's right outside. "Oh, I almost forgot. Daddy wanted me to tell you that he went to the cafeteria for coffee."

"Well, go get Levi so I can see that man," she

said and gave me a little push.

Levi walked in, and Momma's eyes filled with tears when he hugged her. "I know everybody around here's wearing Santa hats, but this isn't where we want you to spend Christmas," he said. "Don't you worry. I'm not planning on it. I've too many things to do. I don't have time to be sick." She patted his hand. "So, how are things in Houston?'

He glanced at me as if he wanted to tell her what we talked about, but I hoped he'd caught the slight head shake and the "no" message in my eyes.

"Things are going well. Still learning my way around the city, and I'm looking for something closer to my office because the traffic is like Baton Rouge during an L.S.U. game. Except it's like that daily. That's a hard one to get used to after a turnaround and five traffic lights in Magnolia Hills." He stood behind me, his hands on the back of the chair where I sat.

"Lord, I'd be fit to be tied." She smoothed her sheets and took a sip of water. "Since you're both here together, I want to apologize—"

Levi held up his hand. "No need, really, Miss Nancy. We're all good."

"No, I might not need to. But I want to. I can't speak for your mother, Levi, but I think we might have had taken our being upset about what happened between the two of you some place it never needed to go. And I acted foolishly, and I'm sure I'll be hearing about it—some of those women keep their big hair just to carry all the gossip around—but like my mother always said, 'If they're talking about you they're leaving someone else alone.'" She yawned. "Excuse me . . . it's not the company, so don't go running off. I just want to tell you both that I'm sorry. And, I'd like to say that no matter what happens between the two of you, I'll accept." She paused and looked at us. "But, I'd be lying."

"I know, Momma. I know," I said and rubbed her hand. I'd never noticed how thin her skin had become. I glanced up at Levi, then back at Momma. "We understand calling off our wedding was difficult for both our families, not just us. And we appreciate your apology. All we want you to do now is come home, cook your famous Shrimp Mirliton for Christmas, and watch you play with that sweet grandbaby."

"Me too, sweetheart. Now, I want you two to give me a hug, and get on out of here. It's getting late, and I know you both have things to do tomorrow. I'll probably be home before you."

We hugged her, and before we walked out, she asked Levi if she'd be seeing him for Christmas.

When he looked at me, I know Momma could not have missed the delight in his face, "Oh, yes ma'am. I'll be there."

Chapter Eighteen

❧

ONE LESSON I LEARNED IN life was to never say, "It can't get any worse than this," because the universe often found a way to prove me wrong. I didn't say that about Momma in the hospital or making a life with Levi, but my world start spinning in a different direction in a matter of days anyway.

On the way home from the hospital, Levi and I stopped at Zea's for dinner since neither one of us remembered if the steaks ever made it back to the refrigerator. I asked him if we could wait to talk to Preston until the Library event was over, and Momma was home. He agreed, but he said he was scheduled to be back in the office by the beginning of the year.

After we'd ordered, Levi leaned over and kissed me softly, his lips barely grazing mine. "Being with you has been the best gift I could ever have for

Christmas. I just wanted you to know that."

"Well, good, because I didn't get you any-thing."

"Not true. You gave me everything I've ever dreamed of having. Including showers where I get to wash your hair and trace the bubbles as they trickle down your spine—"

I put my hand over his mouth. "Holy crap, Levi. People might hear you." I looked over my shoulders, but so far, no one seemed to be paying attention. "Plus, if you keeping talking like that, you're going to have to call the waiter over and pay for two iced teas and salads because we're leaving."

He laughed. "That's the Holly I fell in love with. And I intend to keep falling in love with you."

Even on the ride back, I didn't talk to him about the nagging anxiety of Momma's diagnosis. What if she wasn't fine? How could I possibly leave her? And Daddy would be alone taking care of her.

He parked in front of his mother's house and walked me across the street. "I know you're tired, so I'm not going to stay. I have a feeling my mother's waiting to talk to me since the house is lit up like a firecracker."

I wrapped my arms around his neck. "Like high school all over again, huh? Except that you got to run all the bases."

"A home run out of the ball park." He leaned his forehead on mine. "I love you," he whispered.

"I love you, more," I whispered back. And before he could say anything, and with Mr. Freeman next door outside rearranging his lights for the tenth time, and with the scent of night jasmine surrounding us on the porch, I stood tiptoed and brought my lips to meet his. He tasted like coffee and chocolate, and I couldn't get enough of him. His breath warm and soft. His mouth pressing against mine so hard, when we stopped I touched my lips to see if they felt bruised.

That night I fell asleep holding the pillow that smelled like him, remembering the weight of his body on mine, and how it felt to be consumed with passion once again.

By the next evening, my life had been consumed by a diagnosis so unexpected that, when I heard the words from my father, I sat on the floor holding Levi's pillow from the night before, rocking and sobbing.

I'D BEEN AT the bakery all day with Preston, LamarAnn and Allee. Outside, a flocked tree with green and yellow ornaments, laced with crystal beads and topped with a paper-maiché angel greeted customers who walked through the doors. Oversized grapevine wreaths decorated with candy canes, marshmallows, gum drops, and sprinkles hung from each window from gold mesh ribbons. The inside of the store had been transformed to an *Alice in Wonderland* Christmas. Figurines of the characters from the book were nestled around the store with fluffy Santas and bowls of different colored ornaments.

When I spotted Preston, wearing a headband with reindeer antlers, and singing along with Mariah Carey as he filled the display cases, I cried. I couldn't help it, and I didn't try. It was amazing and beautiful and generous. Preston walked over, picked me up and actually twirled me until I was dizzy.

"What are you doing? You're making me dizzy," I said as he slowed down and I landed on the floor again.

"You stopped crying, didn't you?" He kissed the top of my head. "Welcome back. Not get your apron on, and get your ass to work."

Even though, we'd not officially opened, Allee said people had been streaming in all morning and even the day before while they were decorating. She and LamarAnn wore earrings and necklaces of flashing ornaments and Christmas aprons that, of course, had already been monogrammed with their names. "Girl, when you know people who know people, things happen," LamarAnn explained when I asked her how they pulled everything off, including the aprons with one for me and Preston. She greeted people, most of whom she knew, and sampled right along with them as she bagged and boxed goodies.

"You keep eating like that, and it's going to cost you an extra airline seat when we go to Hawaii in July," Allee said when she passed LamarAnn a tray filled with Pistachio, Hazelnut and Espresso biscotti.

"Hells bells, Allee, that's months from now. I'm starting my bikini workout January first." She checked her calendar app. "That's a Thursday. You have to start diets on Mondays. Make that January fifth."

Allee sighed, rolled her eyes, and motioned me to the back. Trays and boxes filled with desserts covered two fold-out tables. "Here's everything for tonight. We need to be there about six o'clock. LamarAnn, Preston and I are going to handle this."

I started to protest, but she shook her head.

"No, you're absolutely, positively forbidden to come. In fact, we won't even allow you through the damn doors."

Allee had the potential to be one scary bitch, so

I just nodded, kept my mouth shut, and listened.

"Preston has already worked everything out with Levi to make sure your butt doesn't show up here. He's picking you up around five o'clock, and you're going to pick up dinner for your mother and father, so they aren't subjected to another hospital meal."

"But can I ask what tomorrow's plan is?"

"Sure. We're . . . the bakery's closed. Preston decided that no one should ever work Christmas Eve or Christmas day, unless of course they're heathens, and we don't associate with them in Magnolia Hills."

She sounded so serious, I waited for some sign that she meant that to be funny. Allee smiled and wrapped her arms around me. "Thank you for letting us do this for you. Sometimes people just don't want to let themselves be loved."

"Well, they're just heathens, and we don't associate with them, right?"

Chapter Nineteen

ᔈᔇ

I DIDN'T WAIT FOR LEVI to pick me up to go to the hospital. I couldn't call him because I wasn't sure I could even be coherent. So, still wearing my apron from the bakery and clutching my cell phone, I walked across the street and knocked on his door.

Beulah Grace opened the door, looked at me, and called for Levi. "Come here, honey." She brushed my hair out of my face, and my head fell on her shoulder, and I sobbed. "Go ahead. Get it out. I know. I know," she murmured, stroking my hair and swaying as if she was trying to rock me while we stood.

I heard Levi walking down the hallway, and when I opened my eyes, he was walking into the foyer, still wiping shaving cream from his face. Beulah Grace released me when Levi opened his arms, scooped me up and carried me to the couch.

His mother handed him a box of tissues, which he placed on my knees, and she sat next to me, rubbing my back in gentle, soothing circles. I wanted to tell him what my father had said, but my hiccupping between sobs made speaking difficult. When I could breathe, I managed to at least tell them that I'd talked to my father.

Levi placed his hand under my chin and lifted my face toward his. "Okay, take your time," he said, blotting my wet face and eyes with tissues, and handing me a few because I couldn't tell the difference between what was running out of my eyes and what was dripping out of my nose.

At any other time, I might have felt self-conscious making wet honking sounds as I blew my nose. Now, I kept grabbing tissues until nothing was left to expel but air.

Beulah Grace left and came back with a glass of water and two white tablets. "Here, sweetie. Take these. Just pain relievers for the headache you might have soon."

I didn't argue. I swallowed the pills and, after my breathing calmed down, told them what my father had told me.

"My mother has cancer. Ovarian cancer. The doctors think they caught it early enough that all she'll need is a hysterectomy. But, until they do surgery, they won't know exactly what stage it's in and what treatment she'll need after. Like chemotherapy or radiation or maybe both, depending."

Neither Levi nor Beulah Grace said anything yet. The three of us sat together, the shroud of cancer muting all of us.

WHILE LEVI FINISHED getting dressed so we could leave, Beulah Grace apologized for all that had happened between my mother and her. "After Levi left for Houston, and him being devastated when the wedding was called off, I just kind of lost it. Stupid, I realize now. Especially now."

"If it helps any, Momma said the same thing. She's sorry for being so crazy. And not that it's an excuse, but the doctors said that her weight loss and even her weird depression and personality changes made them keep looking beyond a lady who just fainted."

"One thing we can be grateful for is her fainting. If she hadn't . . . well, this could have been so much worse," said Beulah Grace.

"I hadn't thought of that. Momma said the people at the hotel probably thought she'd passed out because she'd never stayed some place so ritzy before." I shook my head. "At least she found a way to laugh about it." As soon as I said "laugh," I thought of Preston, and decided I would video that man laughing come hell or high water if it meant it could help Momma.

Levi told me he'd already called Julie at Maple Street Eatery and ordered four dinners for us to pick up on the way out. I kissed Beulah Grace on the cheek when we left, and I thought she would have been a good mother-in-law after all.

WE PASSED THE Magnolia Hills Library after Levi picked up our dinners, and the parking lot was almost full.

"Looks like they're going to have a good fund-raiser tonight," Levi said.

"I'd be worrying if we had enough desserts, but with Allee at the bakery, they'll probably have too many. Damn. I should have thought to bring some to my parents."

Levi patted my hand. "You were a little pre-occupied. Give yourself a break on that one. We can pick some up tomorrow before we go back."

"Allee said that Preston's closing the bakery tomorrow."

"Oh, that's right . . . but you still have a key don't you?"

"I kept mine, and Preston had extras made for the girls. So, no problem, we can stop and box up enough for the hospital, your parents and Lily's gang at the house. Then again. . .maybe triple J having a sugar rush the night before Christmas won't be on Lily's wish list."

I looked out the car window as we drove to New Orleans and wondered how many times after this I'd need to make this trip to this hospital. The Magnolia Hills Hospital mainly treated broken bones, birthed babies, and had a few outpatient surgeries. If they moved her to MD Anderson Cancer Center in Houston, I'd be able to spend time with Levi. But going there would mean her condition was worse, not better. Not the kind of circumstances I want to have a reason to visit Levi. Momma's diagnosis was changing everything we planned. But, since we hadn't discussed it, I didn't know if Levi had come to that conclusion yet.

"I know you're probably thinking about your Momma, but you're quiet. Scary quiet. What's going on?"

If I said, "Nothing," he knew from past history that usually meant the opposite, so I had to tell him. I wiped my palms on my jeans and thought about how to say what I knew needed to be said.

"Levi, I love you more than I ever thought possible. Being separated from you for months gave me a chance to look at our relationship with a new perspective. At the time, all I could focus on was my broken heart. But, now that you're back, it's all come in focus . . . stronger than before. And

I wanted all our plans to come true. But . . . now, with Momma facing cancer and surgery and treatment . . . I can't leave. Lily's in Baton Rouge, and she has a family and a business, so I wouldn't expect her to travel to Magnolia Hills, and then possibly to New Orleans. If I leave, I'll be six hours away at a time when my parents have no one else to count on for help."

He didn't glance at me or reach out to touch me. "What are you trying to tell me, Holly?"

"I can't marry you, Levi. Not now. I need to be in Magnolia Hills, and not just for the bakery. But for my parents."

Chapter Twenty

❧

SILENCE IS NOT GOLDEN.

Not when you're waiting for your ex-ex-fiancé to react to having heard he's going to be the "ex" again.

If I hadn't emptied myself of tears already, I would have cried.

Levi still didn't respond. I counted three mile-markers and heard nothing. I didn't detect a reaction on his face. His fingers didn't even drum on the steering wheel. "Did you hear me?"

"Yes, I heard you.

"Well?"

"What do want me to say, Holly? She's your mother, and she needs you. I understand. I'd do the same for my own parents. I can't be angry with you because your mother has cancer."

"But I wanted this to work, Levi. I wanted to go back to Houston with you. I still want to, but I can't." I hated feeling helpless and defeated, to be so close to having what I wanted, what we wanted.

"I know. You said that."

I couldn't tell if Levi was acting calmly so that I wouldn't whirl off to some irrational place or if he was disengaged.

"Aren't you upset about this? You're acting as if I read you tomorrow's weather report. I'm confused. I thought you really wanted this too." My internal spring of sanity was getting wound tighter and tighter as Levi became calmer.

"I'm confused, too. Now you're upset because I'm not upset? Would anything change if I raised my voice or begged or cried? I've been here before, remember?"

He glanced at me long enough for me to see the tightness in his face, his lips as tight as his eyes were cold.

"That was mean," I said, almost to myself. He held the trump card, and he played it.

"No, that was true. I don't know what you want to hear."

"Never mind. Nothing." Which meant, of course, everything. I wanted to hear he was disappointed, sad, frustrated. Something. But I guess I didn't know what I wanted to hear either. I found my iPhone, plugged in the ear phones and then popped the pods in my ears. I didn't listen to music or a book or anything but the muffled sound of the car tires as we headed to Tulane Medical Center.

"Hey," Levi grabbed my hand as we walked through the hospital lobby. "Let's not visit your mother while we fighting or whatever this is."

"I'm hurt, not mad. But, whatever. You got over it. I will too."

"Holly," he stepped in front of me. Since he was carrying all the dinners, he couldn't do much more to stop my progress. "Can you put all this crap to the side? Don't bring it to your mother."

"Of course. I'm a star performer. Now, move, so we can get on with this charade, and I can go do my job at the bakery."

Momma looked better than she did the day before. Her hair was brushed and smooth, and even without her entire make-up drawer in front of her, she managed with powder and lipstick she probably kept in her purse. How could someone who looked so pretty and fresh and vibrant be carrying around something so deadly?

Levi shook my father's hand and set the dinners on a table near the door.

I wanted to run to Momma, curl up next to her, and listen to her read me stories. So silly. But the thought of losing her made me realize I needed to savor every minute from this day forward. I already regretted the time I squandered, taking for granted that she'd be around forever.

"Let's have dinner. Let's not talk about ovaries or cancer or surgery or treatment. I want the four of us to have dinner and enjoy it. No tears. No sad faces. No 'if only.' Understand?"

She looked back and forth between the three of us. We nodded obediently.

Levi carried two dinners to my parents. "You must have been hungry because you totally cleared this hospital tray." He opened a box and gave it to my mother, "One broiled trout almandine with crayfish sauce, sweet potato fries, and onion rings."

"Onion rings too?" My father asked.

Momma looked at what he'd ordered. "This from someone who ordered a fried seafood platter with an extra soft shell crab?"

Levi was being so sweet, I wanted to punch him. I had no idea what he'd ordered for me, and it really didn't matter. My stomach was too full of angst and annoyance to eat.

He handed me my dinner. "I'm not that hungry," I said and put the box back on the table. "I'll eat later."

"Well, can you at least check because I think they marked the box wrong." He looked at his open dinner, then back at me.

"Sure. I'd be happy to do that for you," I said

in my bitchiest tone possible and flipped open the box. "Did you order a dinner with an envelope because there's one in here?" I turned it over. My name was on it. "What is this? The restaurant wrote me a note?" I looked at Levi waiting for him to clear the confusion.

"Goodness, Holly, it's not going to open itself by you staring at it." Momma ate a french fry and handed a few to my father.

I handed the dinner back to Levi. "Hold this."

"Sure. I'd be happy to do that for you." He smiled.

"Smart ass," I mouthed.

"Exactly," he said.

Inside the envelope was a flat linen card, edged with cream and gold fleur-de-lis. Simple, but elegant. Something to consider for the bakery as thank-you cards . . .

"Will you read it already?" Momma was taking full advantage of our not being able to get mouthy.

"The firm of Singletary and Tassin is pleased to announce the association of its newest consultant to our New Orleans office effective February 1, 2015 . . . Oh, my God." I wanted to jump up and down like a kid on Christmas morning because this was my Christmas. It was exactly what I wanted. "Is this true? Is this really true?" I waved the card in front of Levi. The expression on his face answered the question for me. I handed the card to my father who read the rest, "Project Consultant Jeremiah Levi Schwartz."

I was so busy kissing Levi that I forgot I was supposed to be mad at him. "Stop one minute."

Levi knew he'd been caught. I could tell by the grin on his face.

"You knew about this the entire ride over here, and you let me think you weren't the least bit upset when I said I couldn't go to Houston."

He nodded. "Guilty"

"So, how long have you known?"

"I interviewed with them a few weeks ago, I didn't know for sure until yesterday. This wasn't the way I planned to tell you, but it seems to be working so far." He graced me with one of his recognizable smirks.

My parents laughed.

"They knew too?"

"Guilty."

"I can't believe you told them before you told me." I tried to pout, but no one bought in. Not even me.

"I had to. I wanted to make sure that I'd be able to do this."

"Do what? Drive me damn crazy? Scheme behind my back?"

Suddenly there was a hush in the room. My

parents weren't even looking at me. I turned to see what they were looking at. There was Levi, in my mother's hospital room, in Tulane Medical Center, surrounded by take-out boxes, on one knee.

He took my hand and asked me that one question I'd always know the answer to. . .again.

"Will you marry me?"

"Yes, yes, yes. As many times as you ask. Yes."

Coming in Early 2015!

Book 2 of The Magnolia Hills Garden Club Series

Finally, the wedding they've all waited for . . . again. Jeremiah Levi Schwartz and Holly Belle Pressfield are tying the knot. They're double-tying it. But if they thought planning the first wedding was challenging, they're finding planning the second first wedding is more complicated than getting Preston, Holly's business partner in the bakery, to the church on time.

Recovering from her surgery, Nancy Jane, Holly's mother, goes to the Annual Garden Club Convention in Mobile, Alabama, with Beulah Grace, Levi's mother. They're not prepared for what being part of the National Garden Club really means. And when the Girls' Night Out gang holds Holly's bachelorette party in Mobile so she can keep track of her mother, who knows what secrets they'll come home with and which ones they'll leave behind.

www.ingramcontent.com/pod-product-compliance
Lightning Source LLC
Chambersburg PA
CBHW070628130626
46555CB00006B/2484